To K and to all the children and adults impacted by domestic violence.

This is a work of fiction. Names, characters, places, and incidents either are the product of the author's imagination or are used fictitiously. Any resemblance to actual persons, living or dead, events, or locales is entirely coincidental.

First paperback edition April 2024

Book cover by Amanda Letcher
Illustrations by Amanda Letcher

ISBN 979-8-9905859-0-4 (paperback)
ISBN 979-8-9905859-1-1 (ebook)

Chameleon and the Color of Brave

Written by Amanda Moore
Illustrated by Amanda Letcher

I am Chameleon.

The coolest thing about me is my skin changes color to match my emotions.

Happy.
Sad.
Angry.
Silly.
Scared.
Confused.
Guilty.

Today I discovered a new color.

The color of Brave.

It starts with my family.
Sometimes it's hard to be home.

Things are okay for a while,

then my dad gets angry.

My sister, Mom, and
I stay out of his way.

!!
But no matter what we do,
he gets angry.
So angry.
Angry

He yells, screams, and breaks stuff. He hurts my mom.

Sometimes he hurts my sister and me.

When that happens, I feel really
Scared.
Confused.
Sad.
Angry.

Sometimes my dad says he's sorry.

He buys my mom flowers and gets my sister and me new toys.

He says he won't get angry or
hurt us again.

But he always gets angry again.
And then he hurts us.

Over and over again.

One day at school I'm thinking
about what happens at home.
I turn all sorts of colors.

I'm **scared** he's going to be angry again.

I'm **angry** that he hurts us.

I feel **guilty** for not keeping my mom and sister safe.

But most of all I feel confused.
So confused.

How can he be so much fun and say he loves us and then hurt us?

My teacher asks if I'm okay.
She says I can tell her anything,
and she'll try to help.

I'm **scared** to tell her
what happens at home.

What if my
dad finds out?
Scared
What would happen
to me? What would
happen to my family?
Confused. Sad. Guilty.

Then I see a tiny spot of a
color I have never seen before.

I feel stronger,
like I can tell her.

Like I have to tell her.

The spot gets bigger

and bigger

and bigger

until I am covered
in this new color.

I tell her everything about
what happens at home.
The anger.
The pain.
The fear.

She tells me what happens at home is not my fault. She says I am brave.

So brave.

And that's how I discovered
the Color of Brave.

I want you to know
that you have the
Color of Brave too.

Even if you cannot see it,
**you have brave
inside of you.**

For Safe Adults:

If the child you are with has been impacted by domestic violence, use the coloring sheet below to help them express how they feel about domestic violence. Remind the child that just like Chameleon felt multiple emotions about the violence, they might feel multiple emotions too. Have the child use Chameleon's color key to color in the emotions that they feel.

For Safe Adults:

The author intentionally left the conclusion of the book open-ended because the response to domestic violence varies greatly. Some children may benefit from "finishing" the story to match what they have experienced or what they would like to have happen after their disclosure.

Use the background scene below and have the child draw (or use the cutouts) to show what happened after Chameleon told his teacher. Print multiple copies if more pages are needed. *(For example, if the child had to talk to police officers, then the child could draw Chameleon talking to the police.)* In the drawings, use Chameleon's color key to show how Chameleon (and the child) felt or might feel in the situation they are drawing.

After Chameleon told his teacher...

AUTHOR

Amanda Moore, MA, LLPC is a children's trauma therapist. You will usually find her in a costume, covered in paint, or in a giant pile of toys as she strives to bring a smile to children's faces as they talk about the trauma they have experienced. She brings this same balance of fun and talking about hard things to her writing. Amanda would love to hear from you.

To connect with the author, email her at amandamooreauthor@gmail.com.

Made in the USA
Las Vegas, NV
08 December 2024